Disney's

READ-TO-ME TREASURY

❧ VOLUME TWO ❧

DISNEY PRESS

NEW YORK

CONTENTS

❧ INTRODUCTION ❧

Swing through the jungle with Tarzan and his family; slurp spaghetti and meatballs with Lady and Tramp; or hop on Bullseye for a ride around Andy's room. . . . You and your child can share these magical adventures and more in this treasury of beloved Disney tales.

Dear Parents and Caregivers:

Educators will tell you that reading aloud to your child for at least fifteen minutes a day is one of the best gifts you can give your child. Not only will you help your child develop language skills, but you will be setting the foundation for a love of books and a desire to read. You will also be spending time with your loved one. What could be better than that?

The Whens and Whys of Reading Aloud

You can read aloud to your child whenever you have the time or whenever a child hands you the book and says, "Please read to me." Bedtime and naptime make a nice routine time for reading. But don't forget to take along a book when you visit the pediatrician or dentist. Reading can be a comforting diversion. For trips on a plane, bus, or train, reading can help pass the time.

Depending on the age of your child, he or she might want to sit with this treasury and flip through the pages, talk aloud to the characters or raise questions about what happens on a particular page. Let your child experience the book in his or her own way. Be around to answer or comment. The more you and your child become involved with the story, the more an appreciation for books, language, and storytelling will grow.

You might ask your child to choose which of the stories he or she would like to hear. Don't be surprised if after reading one tale, your child asks you to reread that same tale again and yet again. Revisiting stories helps young children make connections between the stories they hear and the pictures and words they see. They begin to be able to predict what is going to happen next. Familiarity makes your child an expert—a positive feeling that is then attached to the whole

reading experience. Repetition not only helps children develop a comfort zone with books, but it also reinforces important letter and word recognition skills.

If your child shows an interest in words, you might pause at certain places in the text and ask: Can you find the word that says *Pongo*? Can you find the names of Andy's toys? Associating written words with storytelling is an important reading-readiness skill. But remember to let your child set the pace and tell you what he or she wants to learn or talk about.

Quick Tips

Here are some hints to help you and your little reader on your way:

• Set a reading mood. Let your little listener settle in and, perhaps by looking at the cover, start thinking about the story.

• Children have different attention spans. Note that each of the stories in the treasury is divided into sections, so you have a natural place to stop and then start again at another sitting.

• Put lots of expression into your reading—if possible, change your voice to fit each character.

• Keep your child involved. Invite him or her to turn the pages when it's time.

• At the end of each section, you might raise questions such as: What do you think will happen to Woody? Will he meet up with his pal Buzz again? Will the Dalmatian pups escape Cruella? Why do you think so? Do you think Tarzan will stay with his ape family? Never pry an interpretation from your child. Let your child's interests be your guide.

• Don't rush. A slow-paced read gives your child time to explore the pictures and make their own mental map of what's happening in the story. Plus, it reinforces the message that you enjoy spending quiet time together.

So now it's time to find that cozy nook, to cuddle and snuggle with your child, and to share a Disney read-to-me story together. You're ready to embark on the magical road to reading!

The Editors

5

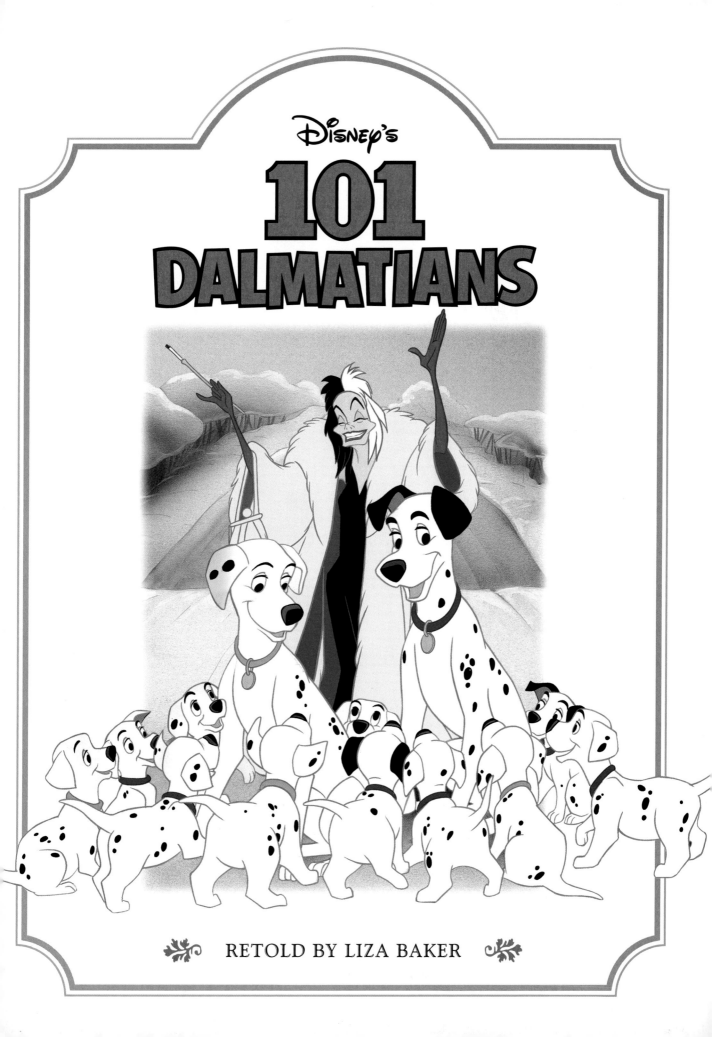

Disney's

101 DALMATIANS

RETOLD BY LIZA BAKER

8

New Beginnings

My story begins in London, where I lived with my pet, Roger Radcliff. Roger was a songwriter and we lived in a bachelor flat near Regent's Park. My name is Pongo. I'm the one with the spots, looking out the window.

As far as I could see, a bachelor's life was downright dull. So when I saw the perfect dog walk by with a lovely woman, it was a dream come true.

I grabbed my leash and barked loudly, "Rrrruff, rrrruff!" Roger understood and took me out.

As I pulled Roger along, he asked me,
"Pongo, old boy. What's the hurry?"

Then I spotted the lovely Dalmatian and her
pet. I slowed down as we walked by, hoping we'd
catch their eye.

13

But when I looked back, they were starting to leave. Thinking fast, I wrapped up Roger and the lovely lady in my leash.

"Ohhhhh! Ohhh dear!" they cried, losing their balance and falling right into a pond. After a moment, they couldn't help but laugh. My plan had worked!

15

Not long after that, Anita and Roger were married.

And I took Perdita to be my bride.

For the first six months, we lived in a small house near the park. It was perfect for two couples just starting out. We even had a wonderful housekeeper named Nanny.

I thought that we couldn't be any happier, but Perdita had the best news yet!

"Oh, Pongo, we're going to have puppies," she announced happily.

One day an old classmate of Anita's, Cruella De Vil, stopped by. "Darling," she asked Anita, "where are the little brutes . . . er, puppies?"

"They won't be here for at least three weeks," replied Anita anxiously.

"Let me know when the Dalmatians arrive. Don't forget!" Cruella demanded.

On a stormy night three weeks later, Nanny cheered, "The puppies are here! All fifteen of them!" Then thunder cracked and Cruella swooped into the room.

"I'm here for the puppies—I'll buy them all!" Cruella sneered. She started to write a check, splattering ink everywhere.

"We're not selling the puppies and that's final!" shouted Roger.

23

Cruella stormed out.

"Perdy, don't worry. We're keeping the puppies," I whispered. "Every last one of them!" Perdita sighed happily and we went to sleep.

Weeks passed, and our fifteen little ones certainly kept us busy! One of the things the puppies liked best was watching the adventures of Thunderbolt the dog on television.

"Bedtime, children," said Perdita when the show was over.

Nanny tucked the puppies in as we left for our nightly walk in the park with Roger and Anita.

Beware Cruella!

Just as Nanny had lulled the little ones off to sleep, the doorbell rang.

Two men, Jasper and Horace, were at the door. "We're here to inspect the . . . uhh . . . wiring," said Jasper. Then the two pushed their way into the house.

"You're not comin' in here!" shouted Nanny. "I'll call the police!" But before she could do anything, they locked her in her room.

When Nanny finally escaped, she made a terrible discovery. The puppy basket was empty!

"They took the puppies!" she sobbed, hurrying off to find the police.

I knew that Cruella must have chuckled when she read the morning's newspaper headline: FIFTEEN PUPPIES STOLEN—THIEVES FLEE. Her plan had worked!

That evening in the park, I said to Perdita, "It's up to us to find the puppies." We decided to use the Twilight Bark, an all-dog alert. I barked as loudly as I could.

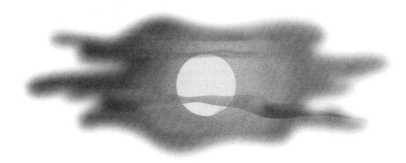

The news traveled quickly out to the country, where a bloodhound named Towser heard the shocking story. "Ruff! Ruff!" he barked, trying to reach the Colonel, an Old English sheepdog that lived nearby.

Towser's message reached the Colonel and his friends. Then Sergeant Tibs the cat said, "I heard puppies barking at the old De Vil place two nights ago."

The friends decided to investigate the mansion. Sergeant Tibs sneaked through a hole in the wall and found a room . . . overflowing with Dalmatian puppies!

The fifteen missing puppies were there, but they weren't alone. Jasper and Horace had brought a total of ninety-nine puppies to the house!

Sergeant Tibs hid when he heard Cruella arrive. She screamed at Jasper and Horace, "I don't care how you kill the spotted beasties! I want my coats tonight!"

Then she stormed out to her car and sped away. Sergeant Tibs couldn't believe his ears. Cruella wanted the puppies for fur coats!

Immediately, Sergeant Tibs ran inside to round up the puppies. "You'd better get out of here," he whispered. Then he helped them escape through a hole in the wall.

Suddenly Horace and Jasper noticed that the puppies were missing.

"Follow me!" cried Sergeant Tibs, hiding the pups beneath the staircase.

Horace and Jasper ran after them calling, "Here, puppies. Here, puppies."

Meanwhile, Perdita and I had sneaked out of our house. Thanks to the dogs in London, we heard what had happened and began our journey to the De Vil mansion.

When we arrived at last, we found the Colonel standing in front of the gate. "Follow me," he said, heading to the house. "I'm afraid there's trouble! Big hullabaloo!"

Through the window we
saw that Horace and Jasper had
cornered the puppies.
Perdita and I broke through the
glass with a *crash* and surprised the
evil men. Those dognappers were
no match for us!

We gathered the puppies and escaped from the
mansion to a nearby barn. But we didn't realize that
Jasper and Horace were hot on our trail!

Puppies, Puppies, Puppies

In the barn, we counted up all the puppies. There were ninety-nine! Without hesitating I said, "We'll take them all home with us. Every last one of them."

Suddenly we heard a truck screech outside. It was Horace and Jasper! "You'd better be away!" said the Colonel. "I'll stay behind to fend them off."

"Come on, kids, hurry!" cried Perdita as we made our escape into the snowy night.

The thieves escaped from the Colonel and Sergeant Tibs and followed our tracks in the snow. Sliding across an icy creek, we hid beneath a bridge. Finally, they drove off.

Our long journey continued. Just when we thought we couldn't take another step, we ran into a helpful collie. "We have shelter for you at a dairy farm," he said.

At the barn, four cows
offered our grateful puppies
warm milk, and the collie was
kind enough to bring Perdy
and me scraps to eat. Worn
out, we slept soundly that
night.

In the morning, we rounded up our puppies and headed for Dinsford, where a Labrador was waiting to help us.

As we ducked beneath a fence and crossed a road, I heard a car horn honking in the distance. "Hurry, kids! Hurry!" I said, shooing them along.

Cruella's car came roaring up the road. She screeched to a halt near our tracks in the snow.

Jasper and Horace pulled up next to her in their truck.

Cruella cried, "Their tracks are heading for the village. I'll take the main road, you take the side roads."

At Dinsford, the black Labrador announced that he had found us a ride to London! While we waited in a blacksmith's shop, I came up with a disguise to fool Cruella.

"Come on, kids," I ordered them. "Roll in the ashes!" Soon we all looked like black Labradors!

When our ride was ready, we began
leading the disguised puppies out to the
truck. Cruella and her henchmen didn't
even glance our way.

But as we were helping the last little ones
onto the truck, some melted snow fell on one of the
pups. His spotted coat was revealed!

Cruella yelled, "There they go!"

Our truck sped off and Cruella raced after us, smashing into us at every turn. She was trying to force us off the cliff!

Then Horace and Jasper's truck came speeding toward us from the other direction. Our driver quickly swerved out of the way, and Cruella's car crashed into Horace and Jasper's truck. The three villains tumbled down the cliff and into a snowbank.

At long last, we made it back to London. Roger and Anita hugged and cleaned us as we walked through the door.

We were all so happy to be together again!

As Nanny cleaned off our puppies, she giggled, "Oh, they're all here, the little dears!" That was when she noticed there were many, many more of us.

"Look!" Nanny cried joyously. "There are a whole lot more puppies!" Yes, indeed, there were.

When they had finished counting us, Roger said
in amazement, "There are a hundred and one
Dalmatians! Let's buy a big place in the country and
have a . . . Dalmatian Plantation!"
And that's exactly what we did!

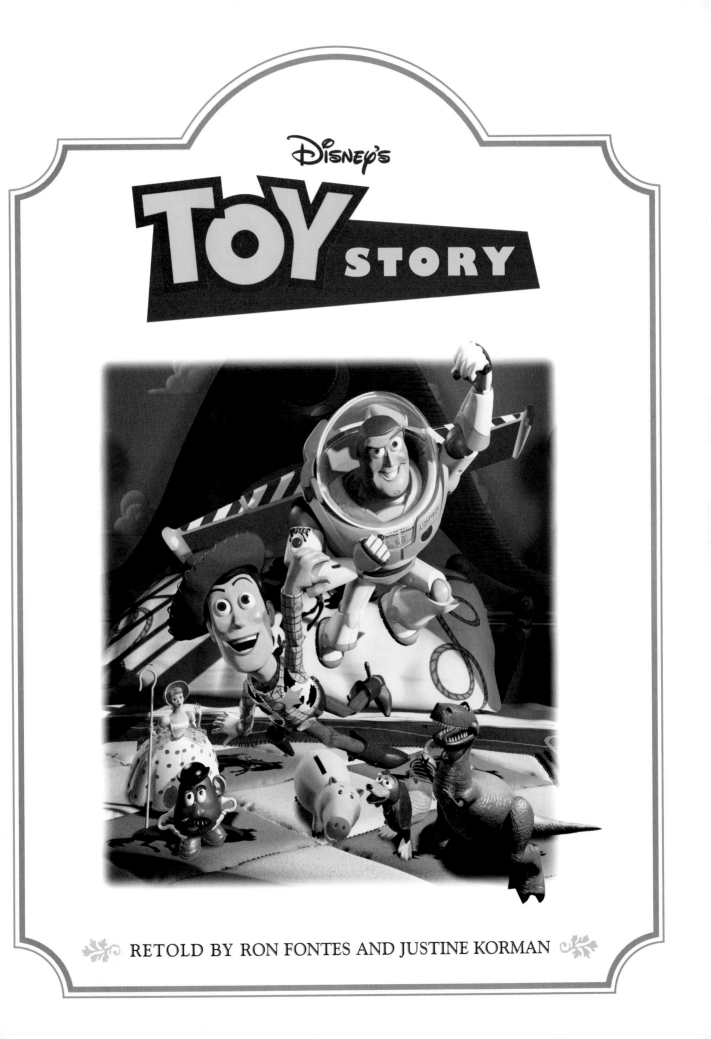

DISNEY'S

TOY STORY

RETOLD BY RON FONTES AND JUSTINE KORMAN

THE BIRTHDAY PARTY

"Reach for the sky! You're going to jail, one-eyed Bart!" cried Andy.

Then Andy pulled the string and Woody said, "You're my favorite deputy." The brave cowboy was Andy's favorite toy.

Andy's mom called from downstairs, "Okay, birthday boy. Go get your sister. It's almost time for your party."

When Andy left the room, his toys came to life!

"Pull my string! The birthday party's today," Woody exclaimed, jumping up. "Okay, everybody, it's clear!"

Andy had many toys: Hamm the piggy bank, Rex the timid dinosaur, Bo Peep and her sheep, the Green Army Men, RC the radio-controlled car, and more!

Woody called a meeting. Andy's family was moving in a week, and Woody wanted to make sure that none of Andy's toys would get lost. But that wasn't their only worry. Birthdays meant new toys for Andy to love, and someone might get replaced!

Woody sent the Green Army Men to spy on the birthday party. The sergeant said, "Code red, men. Recon plan Charlie. Move!"

The soldiers reported that Andy got a lunch box, bedsheets, and a board game. The toys cheered!

"Nothing to worry about," said Woody.
Then Andy's mom brought out a surprise present!
"It's a huge package . . . it's a . . . " Before the
sergeant could finish his report, Andy and his
friends raced up to his room. The toys froze.

Andy tossed his new toy on the bed—in Woody's spot! The cowboy fell to the floor. Then the children left to play games.

Woody dusted himself off and told the other toys, "Let's give whatever it is up there a nice, big, Andy's room welcome."

The new toy was Buzz Lightyear, space ranger! He came in a fancy box shaped like a spaceship.

Buzz activated his wrist-communicator and said, "Buzz Lightyear to Star Command, come in. Do you read me?"

Buzz thought he'd crash-landed on a strange planet. When Woody greeted the new arrival, Buzz fired his laser at the "alien."

"Whoa! I didn't meant to frighten you," Woody said. "I'm Woody and this is Andy's room. And there's been a bit of a mix-up—the bed is my spot."

The other toys crept up on the bed. They were impressed by Buzz. "He's got more gadgets on him than a Swiss Army knife," said Bo Peep.

"You're just a toy. T-O-Y," Woody explained to Buzz. "Your laser is just a blinky light and you can't fly."

94

"Of course I can fly," replied the space ranger. Then he leaped off the bed, shouting, "To infinity and beyond!" Buzz swooped around the room.

Woody scoffed, "That wasn't flying. That was just falling with style."

LOOK OUT FOR SID!

One day, the toys heard a cruel laugh. They looked next door and saw Sid, Andy's mean neighbor, blowing up a toy soldier.

"What's going on?" Buzz wondered.

"Sid tortures toys just for fun!" Rex explained.

Later, Andy's mom told Andy it was time for dinner at Pizza Planet—and Andy could bring only one toy. Woody wanted to be that toy, so he tried to push Buzz behind the desk. But Buzz wound up falling out the window!

The other toys were angry at Woody's careless prank.

99

Andy couldn't find Buzz, so he took Woody. But Buzz managed to scramble into the car, too.

"You're alive! I'm saved," Woody cried.

Woody couldn't wait to bring Buzz home to prove that he wasn't a villain. But at Pizza Planet, Buzz saw a spaceship and rushed inside. The spaceship was really a claw game full of alien toys.

Woody tried to get Buzz out, but it was too late!
Someone was already working the game's claw.
"Gotcha!" cried Sid, as he plucked a tiny alien.

Then Sid pulled out the space ranger! Woody struggled to save Buzz, but wound up getting pulled out of the spaceship, too.

"Awright! Double prizes!" Sid crowed. "Let's go home and play." Sid had a scary gleam in his eyes.

Sid's room was a nightmare of mangled, mutant playthings. Woody and Buzz watched in horror as Sid's dog, Scud, chewed on the tiny alien. Then Sid "operated" on his sister's favorite doll.

"I am outta here!" Woody cried.

Buzz and Woody tried to escape. But Scud was sleeping in front of the door. Suddenly, the dog woke up!

While Scud chased the toys, Woody hid in the closet.

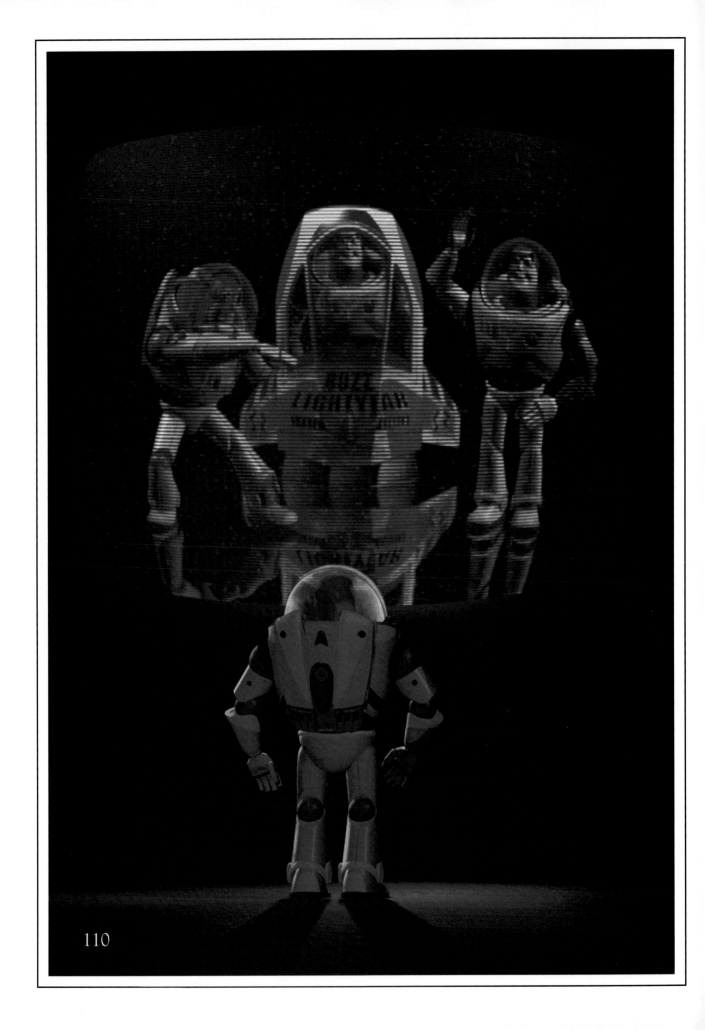

At that moment, Buzz saw a Buzz Lightyear commercial on TV. Now Buzz knew the truth: he *was* a toy!

The space ranger tried one last time to fly, but ended up at the bottom of the stairs with his left arm broken. Dejected, he didn't even care when Sid's sister dressed him up for her tea party.

As soon as the little girl left her room, Woody rushed to Buzz's rescue. "You've had enough tea. Let's get out of here," he said.

Buzz moaned, "I'm a sham. I can't even fly out the window."

"Out the window! Buzz, you're a genius!" Woody exclaimed. He threw a string of Christmas lights from Sid's window to Andy's. They were saved!

But the toys in Andy's room remembered that Woody had made Buzz fall out the window. They weren't about to help a villain. They dropped the lights.

Back in Sid's room, the mutant toys had just fixed Buzz's arm when Sid came in the room with a fireworks rocket. He strapped it to Buzz! Luckily the launch was delayed by rain.

Sid grinned. "Tomorrow's forecast: sunny." Buzz was doomed!

117

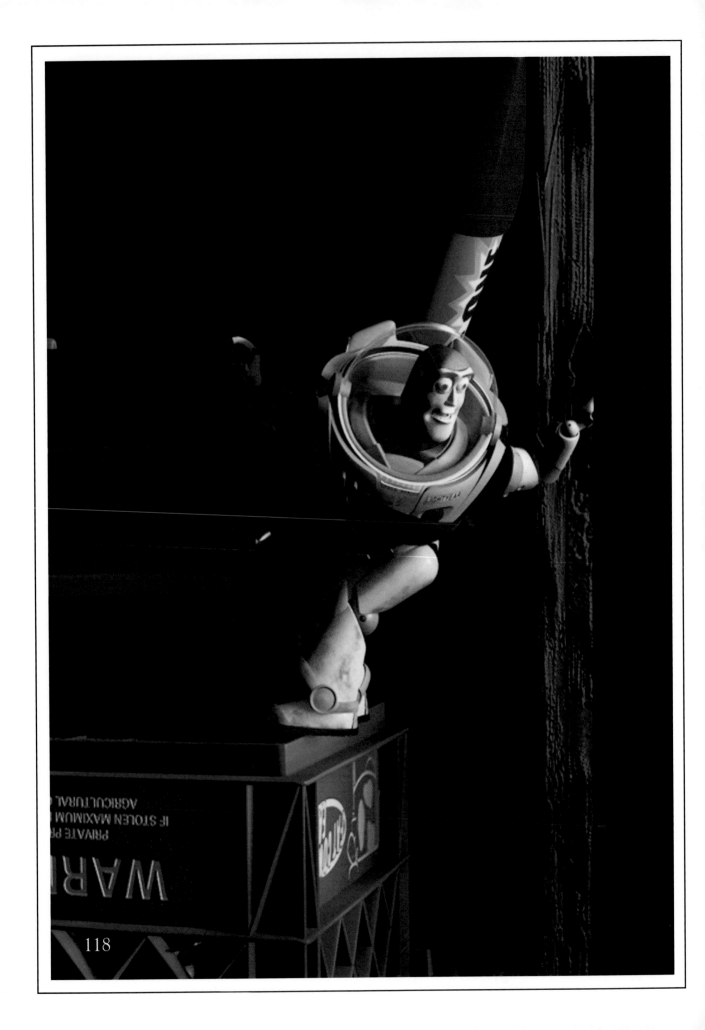

Blast Off!

After Sid went to bed, Woody called out, "Buzz, I need you!" Woody was trapped under a crate.

"I can't help," Buzz replied. "I'm just a toy."

"Any toy would give up his moving parts just to be you!" Woody said. "Andy thinks you're the greatest!"

Buzz thought about Andy and the fun they'd had. "Let's go. There's a kid who needs us."

Just as Buzz freed Woody, Sid woke up! "Time for liftoff!" Sid yelled, and he took Buzz outside.

"There's a good toy out there that's going to be blown to bits. We've got to help him!" Woody told the mutant toys. "Please."

Following Woody's
plan, the toys took
positions in Sid's
backyard.

Sid picked up a match
to light Buzz's rocket and
started the countdown.

123

Just as the match touched the fuse, Sid heard
someone say, "Reach for the sky!" Sid turned in
surprise. Woody was talking, but he hadn't pulled
the toy's string!

"I'm talking to you, Sid," Woody told the surprised
boy. "We don't like being blown up or smashed or
ripped apart."

"W-w-w-we?" Sid gasped.

"Your toys," Woody replied.

The mutant toys moved in on their former tormentor, and Sid ran screaming into his house.

Woody thanked the mutant toys. Then he heard Andy's mother say, "Bye, house." Andy's family was moving!

Buzz and Woody watched as Andy's car drove away. Pursued by Scud, Woody and Buzz ran to catch the moving van. To save Woody, Buzz jumped onto Scud's nose. Now Woody was safely on the van, but Buzz was left behind on the street!

Woody dug RC out of a box and tossed the radio car onto the street. He could use RC to bring Buzz back. But the other toys still thought that Woody had betrayed Buzz. They threw Woody off the truck!

Then the toys saw Buzz in the street. "Woody was telling the truth," said Bo Peep. The toys watched as Woody, Buzz, and RC raced toward the van.

But RC's batteries ran down! Suddenly, Buzz had an idea. "The rocket!"

Woody used Buzz's helmet to focus sunlight, and fired up the rocket's fuse.

FOOSH! The sizzling rocket soared into the sky! Woody managed to drop RC into the van.

"Hey, Buzz, you're flying." Woody laughed.

"I'm just falling with style," Buzz replied, smiling.

"Uh, Buzz? We missed the truck," Woody pointed out.

"We're not aiming for the truck," Buzz said, diving into the car. The toys landed in the box next to Andy!

After that, all was well in Andy's new home—until Christmas, which meant new toys. On Christmas Day, the anxious toys listened to the Green Army Men's report.

"You aren't worried, are you?" Woody teased Buzz. "What could Andy possibly get that is worse than you?" From downstairs came the sound of barking. Andy happily exclaimed, "Wow! A puppy!"

DISNEY'S
TARZAN ®

RETOLD BY VICTORIA SAXON

THE APE MOTHER

A baby's cry drew Kala away from her ape family. The cry was coming from a strange house, high up in a tree's branches.

Inside the house, Kala found the baby. When she held him, he stopped crying and began to laugh with her.

Suddenly, Sabor, a ferocious leopard, sprang at them. Kala risked her own life to save the baby.

Kala brought the baby to her family.
"You cannot keep it," said Kerchak, the apes'
leader. "It's not our kind."

"Sabor killed his family," Kala explained.

Reluctantly, Kerchak agreed to let her raise
the child. Kala named the baby Tarzan.

As he grew, Tarzan tried to fit in with his ape family. "I'd love to hang out with you," his friend Terk told Tarzan. "But the guys, they need a little convincing."

"What do I gotta do?" asked Tarzan gamely.

"Well you gotta . . . uh . . . go get an elephant hair," Terk said.

To Terk's surprise, Tarzan leaped from the cliff and swam toward the huge creatures!

When Tarzan grabbed an elephant's tail, all the elephants began to trumpet and scramble about in fear. They started to stampede!

The charging elephants rushed through the apes' feeding area. Kerchak leaped to rescue a baby ape just in time.

At the water's edge, Terk ran to Tarzan. "Come on, buddy!" she cried. "Don't die on me." As Tantor, a baby elephant, looked on worriedly, Tarzan revived.

Then Kerchak arrived. Tarzan took all the blame for the stampede.

"Tarzan will never fit into this family," Kerchak shouted at Kala.

That evening, Tarzan knelt at the edge of a pool and looked at his reflection. Kala approached.

"Why am I so different?" Tarzan asked, placing his hands against Kala's.

Kala gently put her son's head to her heart. "Inside we're the same," she said. "Kerchak just can't see that."

Tarzan smiled. "I'll make him see it," he said. "I'll be the best ape ever!"

As Tarzan grew, he learned to swim like the hippos, swing from vines like the monkeys, and surf along mossy tree limbs.

And when Sabor attacked the apes, Tarzan swung to the rescue with his spear and saved Kerchak's life! Tarzan lifted the slain leopard and let out a victory yell.

Respectfully, Tarzan laid the slain leopard at Kerchak's feet.

Then, a gunshot rang out! Kerchak hurried the apes deeper into the jungle, but Tarzan was curious. He searched for the creature that had made the strange noise.

Strangers in the Jungle

From a treetop, Tarzan studied the first humans he had ever seen.

"Mr. Clayton, your gunshots may be scaring off the gorillas," said Jane to her guide.

"Look! A gorilla nest!" exclaimed Professor Porter, Jane's father. Porter and Clayton pressed on, looking for more nests.

As Jane sketched a baby baboon, the small creature grabbed the picture from her. Jane snatched it back and a group of angry baboons began to chase her.

She turned and ran from the mob when . . . whoosh! Tarzan swooped her into the air.

Safe at last, Tarzan looked at Jane intently. Then he placed his hand against hers. She was like him!

Tarzan pointed to himself. "Tarzan," he said.

"Jane," she replied, pointing to herself.

"Jane," Tarzan repeated, smiling.

165

Meanwhile, Terk, Tantor, and their friends had found the humans' camp. Terk touched the typewriter. Another ape dropped a plate. The new sounds were fun!

"I feel something happenin' here!" cried Terk. She was rollicking to an all-out jam session when Tarzan and Jane arrived.

When Tarzan led Jane into the camp, she was surprised to see how he greeted Terk. "He's one of them!" Jane gasped. Then an angry Kerchak arrived and Tarzan had to leave with his gorilla family.

Kerchak ordered the gorillas to stay away from the strangers.

Tarzan objected, "They mean us no harm!" Then Tarzan turned to his mother. "Why didn't you tell me there were others like me?" he asked. But Kala did not answer him.

171

The next day, Tarzan returned to the humans' camp.

Tarzan fascinated Professor Porter. "He moves like an ape but looks like a man!" Porter exclaimed.

Jane and her father taught Tarzan about the human world. Tarzan, who could imitate almost any animal in the jungle, was now quickly learning English.

Tarzan showed Jane his world, too.

One day when Tarzan arrived at the camp, he realized that Jane was leaving. The boat had arrived to take her back to England.

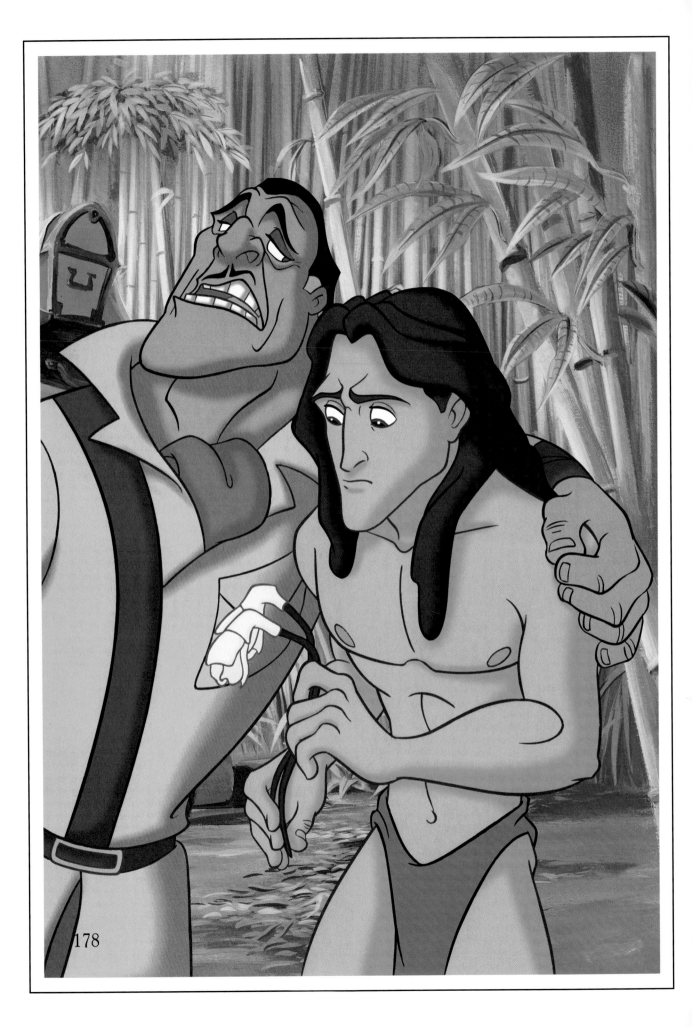

Clayton told Tarzan, "If only she could have spent time with the gorillas . . ."

"Then Jane would stay?" Tarzan asked. Clayton nodded, smiling slyly.   "I'll do it," said Tarzan.

So Terk and Tantor distracted Kerchak while Tarzan led Jane and the others to meet his ape family.

TWO WORLDS MEET

Jane and Porter loved the apes at first sight.

Tarzan spoke to the apes. "Oo-oo-ee-eh-ou."

Jane repeated his sounds and the baby apes cheered. "What did I say?" she asked.

"That Jane stays with Tarzan," he replied with a grin.

Then Kerchak returned—just as Clayton began arguing with a gorilla. Enraged, Kerchak leaped to protect the gorilla from Clayton.

"Run!" Tarzan shouted. He tackled Kerchak while the humans escaped.

183

"You betrayed us all!" Kerchak told Tarzan.

Kala saw that Tarzan was torn between his love for his ape family and his need to be with the humans. Though she risked losing him forever, she led him to the tree house where she had found him.

Tarzan dressed in his father's clothes. Embracing Kala, he said, "No matter where I go, you will always be my mother."

Tarzan ran to the beach to catch up with Jane. Boarding the ship, Tarzan cast a sad glance back at his jungle home.

"Tarzan!" Jane cried in warning. But it was too late. Clayton and his evil companions ambushed Tarzan.

189

Clayton revealed his terrible plan. He wanted to capture the gorillas and sell them! Tarzan yelled in anguish—he had betrayed his family.

Tarzan's cry echoed deep in the jungle. Hearing it, Tantor charged to the rescue with Terk in tow!

With a crash, Tantor broke through the ship's deck, freeing Tarzan and the others. Tarzan swung quickly to the ape's nesting area, but Clayton had already captured Kerchak.

As Tarzan freed him, Kerchak said, "You came back."

"No, I came home," Tarzan replied.

Jane and Porter arrived with Terk and Tantor. Jane swung down on a vine and knocked one of Clayton's thugs aside.

"I'm going to have you out of this in a second," she told Kala.

As Jane freed Kala, a shot rang out. Clayton had shot Tarzan in the arm! Clayton fired again, but this time Kerchak leaped between Tarzan and the bullet.

Wounded, the large ape fell to the ground. Now it was up to Tarzan to protect his family. Tarzan led Clayton up into the tall jungle trees.

Lunging at Tarzan, Clayton fell to his death.
Tarzan ran back to Kerchak. "Forgive me," Tarzan said.
With his final words, Kerchak told Tarzan, "Take
care of our family, my son."

The next day Tarzan and Jane said good-bye.

Rowing toward the ship, Porter said, "Jane, dear, I can't help feeling that you should stay. You love him."

Jane knew her father was right. She jumped out of the boat—and so did Porter!

"Oo-oo-ee-eh-ou," Jane said. She and her father were staying.

They were welcomed to their new home by all the apes . . . and by Tarzan, who knew at last where he belonged.

Walt Disney's

Lady and the TRAMP

❧ RETOLD BY DEBBIE WEISSMANN ❧

Lady

"**M**erry Christmas, Darling!" said Jim Dear as he handed his wife a pink striped box. Inside was a little brown puppy.

Darling took one look at the puppy and decided to call her Lady.

Lady was happy in her new home. She slept in the same room with Jim Dear and Darling.

She romped in the yard and kept watch over the house.

When Lady was older, Jim Dear and Darling gave her a collar with a name tag. Lady proudly showed her collar to her friends Jock and Trusty.

"She's a full-grown lady," said Jock.

211

Tramp was another dog who was sometimes in the neighborhood. He didn't have a warm home and family. He liked to wander the streets, looking for scraps and helping his friends escape the dogcatcher.

Tramp overheard Jock and Trusty telling Lady that Jim Dear and Darling were expecting a baby.

"What's a baby?" Lady asked.

"Just a cute little bundle of trouble," said Tramp. Lady's life was about to change.

The Baby

One rainy April day, the baby came. Jim Dear and Darling were thrilled with their new little boy. Lady liked the baby, too.

Jim Dear and Darling decided to take a trip. Aunt Sarah came to look after the baby. Her two cats came, too. Aunt Sarah was not very nice to Lady.

Her two cats were not very nice, either. They made a mess of the house and pretended that Lady caused the trouble.

"Oh, that wicked animal!" said Aunt Sarah.

Aunt Sarah took Lady straight to the pet store.
"I want a good, strong muzzle," Aunt Sarah said.
The muzzle scared Lady. She jumped off the
counter and ran out the door.

She ran and ran. Soon some big, mean dogs started to chase after her. Lady was scared. Luckily, Tramp heard all the barking and raced to Lady's rescue.

226

"Oh, poor kid," said Tramp, looking at Lady's muzzle. "We've gotta get this off. Come on."
Tramp took Lady to the zoo. Maybe one of the animals could help Lady.

The apes, the alligator, and the hyena were no help at all. Then Lady and Tramp found the beaver. He loved to chew and soon bit right through the muzzle strap.

"It's off!" Lady said with relief.

The beaver was happy, too. He could use the muzzle as a handy-dandy log puller.

Then Tramp took Lady to supper at Tony's Restaurant. Tramp's friend Tony liked Lady and fed the pair his specialty—spaghetti with meatballs!

Tramp and Lady accidentally ate the same spaghetti noodle. Next thing they knew, they were kissing! Lady and Tramp were falling in love.

The happy pair walked to the top of a hill. They gazed up at the full moon that shone over their town. It was a beautiful night.

The next morning, on the way home, Tramp and Lady
passed a chicken coop.

"Ever chased chickens?" Tramp asked. He couldn't resist
Lady did not like the idea, but she followed him anyway.

The chickens ran around the yard squawking and squealing.

"Hey, what's going on in there?" the farmer called.

241

Lady and Tramp ran away as fast as they could.
But Tramp soon discovered that Lady wasn't behind
him. She had run into the dogcatcher and was
brought to the dog pound!

Lady was scared to be at the dog pound. But soon the dogcatcher came for her. Reading her collar, he found out where she lived. "You're too nice a girl to be in this place," he said, and returned Lady to Aunt Sarah.

At home, Aunt Sarah chained Lady to the doghouse. Lady was so sad, even Jock and Trusty could not cheer her up.

Then Tramp arrived. Lady was angry with him.
She thought Tramp had only looked out for
himself and had let her get caught.

He tried to explain. "I thought you were right behind me, honest," he said.

"Good-bye. And take this with you," Lady said, returning the bone Tramp had brought for her.

Tramp

Soon Lady saw a rat creeping into the baby's room. She couldn't chase it because of the chain. She could only bark. "Stop that!" Aunt Sarah called. "Hush."

But Tramp heard and rushed back to Lady.

"What is it?" Tramp asked.

"A rat in the baby's room," Lady replied.

Tramp ran into the house and found the rat.

He had to catch that rat before it hurt the baby.

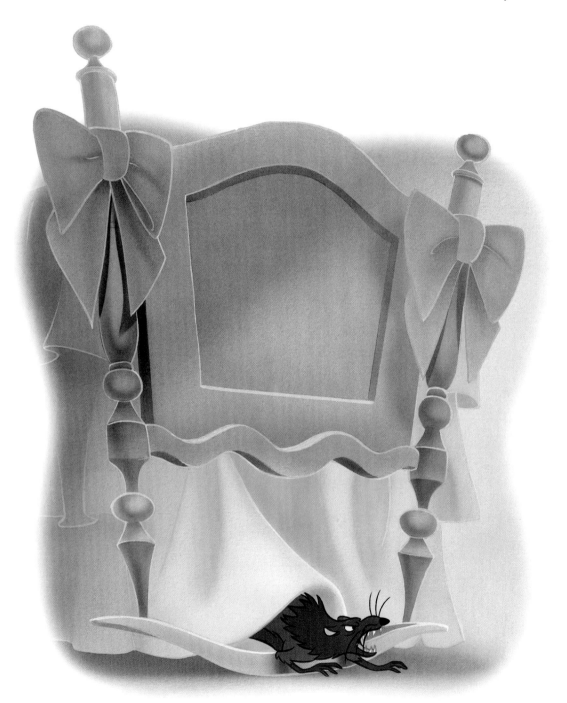

Meanwhile, Lady was barking with all her might and pulling on the heavy chain. At last the chain broke free from the doghouse. Lady ran inside to help Tramp.

Tramp chased the rat under the baby's bassinet and accidentally knocked it over. The baby started to cry. But Lady was happy because the baby was safe—Tramp had finally caught the rat.

Aunt Sarah was not happy. The baby's crying woke her, and she found Lady and Tramp in his room. She thought they were hurting the baby. She called the dogcatcher to come for Tramp.

The dogcatcher soon arrived.

Just then, Jim Dear and Darling came home. Lady tried to explain what happened. She lifted the curtain to show that Tramp had caught the rat and saved the baby.

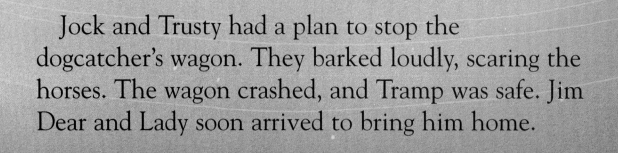

Jock and Trusty had a plan to stop the dogcatcher's wagon. They barked loudly, scaring the horses. The wagon crashed, and Tramp was safe. Jim Dear and Lady soon arrived to bring him home.

The next Christmas Eve, Jock and Trusty came
by to see Lady, Tramp—and their four new puppies.
"They've got their mother's eyes," said Trusty.
"There's a bit of their father in them, too," said
Jock.

Everyone was happy that Tramp
had become part of the family.

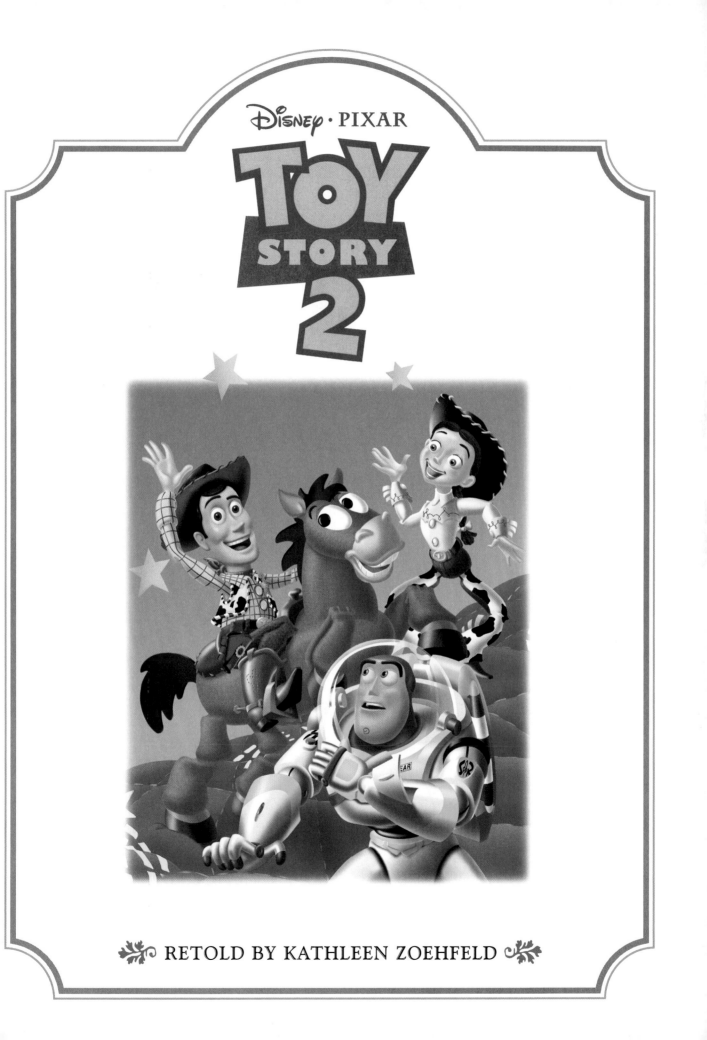

272

WOODY GETS STOLEN

When his arm tore, Woody couldn't go to Cowboy Camp with Andy.

"Woody's been shelved!" cried Mr. Potato Head.

The next morning, Sarge yelled, "Red alert!" Andy's mom was having a yard sale.

When a toy penguin was taken to the sale, Woody rode Andy's puppy to the rescue!

But as the puppy ran back to the house, Woody fell to the ground!

Helplessly, Buzz Lightyear watched a toy collector steal Woody and drive away.

At the collector's apartment, Woody met
Bullseye the horse and Jessie the cowgirl.
"And say hello to the Prospector," said Jessie.
"He's mint in the box. Never been opened."

279

"It's good to see you, Woody," said the Prospector.

"How do you know my name?" asked Woody. Then he saw his own face on the cover of a magazine.

When Jessie put a tape in the VCR, an announcer hollered, "Welcome to *Woody's Roundup!*" Woody had been a TV star!

BUZZ TO THE RESCUE

Back home, Buzz, Slinky, Mr. Potato Head, Hamm, and Rex set out to rescue Woody. They had recognized the man who stole Woody from a TV commercial.

"To Al's Toy Barn and beyond!" declared Buzz.

Woody was having fun playing with his new friends, but they all froze when Al walked into the room.

Al was gloating about how much money he could sell Woody for, when . . . *RIP!* Woody's arm tore off!

Woody was still determined to get home. When Al fell asleep, he tried to escape.

BLARE! The television blasted on. Woody froze as Al woke up. Then Woody noticed the TV remote control. Had one of his new friends turned on the TV?

By that time, Buzz and the others had reached a busy, four-lane highway. "We have to find a way to cross," said Buzz.

Five orange traffic cones trotted across, sending the traffic every which way.

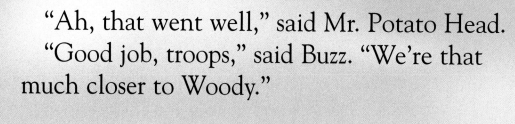

"Ah, that went well," said Mr. Potato Head. "Good job, troops," said Buzz. "We're that much closer to Woody."

290

Al hired a cleaner to fix Woody's arm and make him look like new.

"You'll be a perfect museum piece," said Al.

Down one aisle, Buzz discovered—a new Buzz!
"You're breaking ranks, Ranger," declared the new
Buzz. When they tussled, the new Buzz twist-tied
Andy's Buzz in a box and crammed him on the shelf.

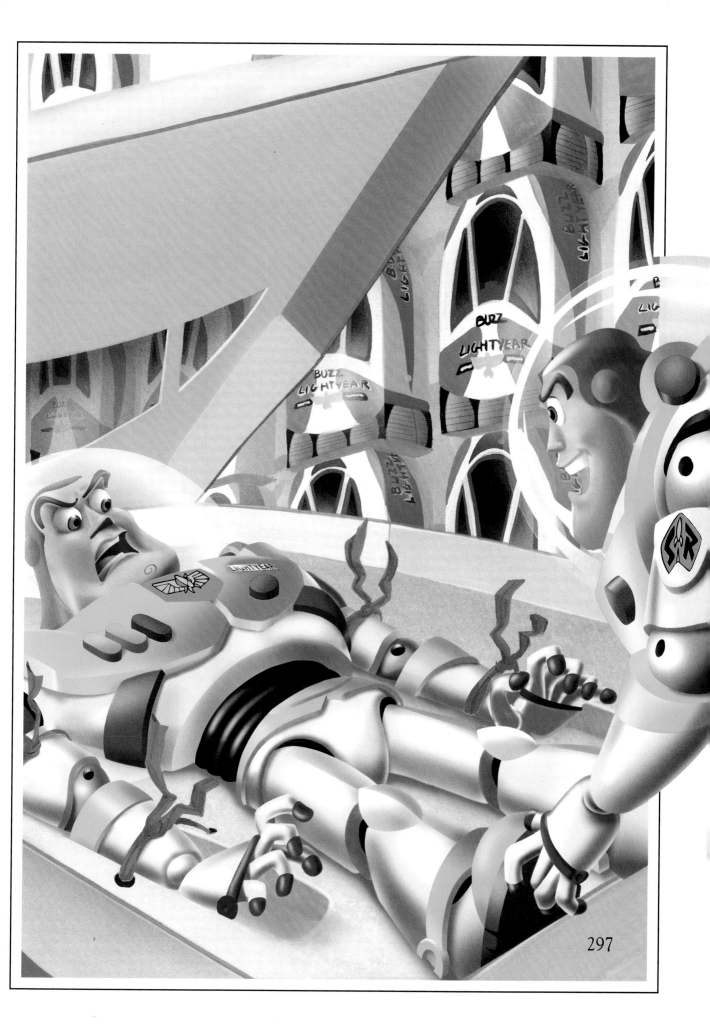

297

298

Soon the other toys arrived
in a sports car. "I found a manual
that shows how to defeat Zurg!" said
Rex, talking about the video game he
could never win.

"Let's go!" shouted the new Buzz—he was
ready to battle Zurg for the safety of the universe!

The toys headed for Al's office. They heard Al planning to sell Woody to a museum in Japan!

The toys hid in Al's briefcase just before Al got ready to leave.

Andy's Buzz escaped from the box and hurried after Al. Buzz didn't notice that a Zurg toy had burst out of its box and was following him!

The toys followed Al into his apartment building. "We can climb through here," said the new Buzz, pointing to an air vent. Finally, the toys broke through the vent leading into Al's apartment!

"We're here to spring you, Woody!" cried Slinky.

Then Andy's Buzz arrived. To prove that he was the real Buzz, he lifted his boot. In thick black marker on the bottom was the name ANDY!

"Let's go, Woody," said Buzz.

To his surprise, Woody said, "I'm a rare collectible. I belong in a museum."

"You . . . are . . . a . . . toy!" Buzz shouted, but Woody refused to leave.

As the toys left, Woody thought about his old life. "I'm supposed to be played with," he decided. "I have to get home!" But the Prospector stood in his way.

From the vent, Buzz watched as Al returned and packed Woody in his bag.

"We gotta get Woody! He changed his mind!" cried Buzz. But the toys ran right into . . . Zurg!

A battle broke out between the Buzzes and Zurg.

As Rex turned away, his tail knocked Zurg into the elevator shaft. "I finally defeated Zurg!" cheered Rex.

The toys said good-bye to the new Buzz, who had decided to stay behind with Zurg.

As they left the building, they saw Al's car pulling away. Mr. Potato Head found them a vehicle of their own. "Pizza, anyone?" he said, smiling.

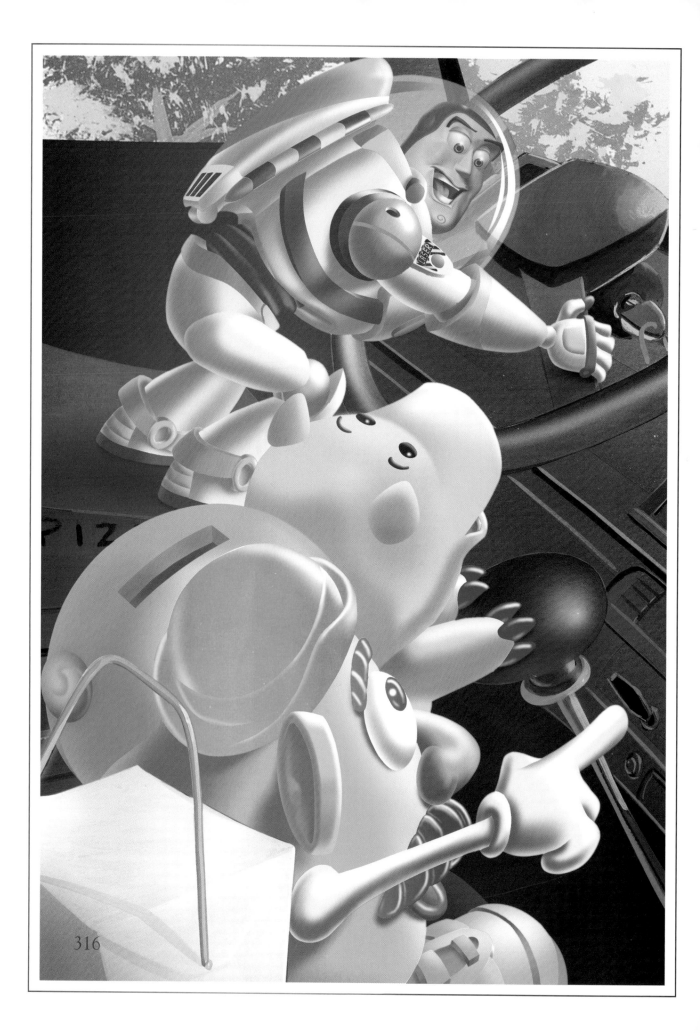

THE AIRPORT CHASE

Barreling down the highway in a Pizza Planet truck, the toys followed Al all the way to the airport.

As Al headed into the terminal, Buzz spotted a pet carrier. "There's the perfect camouflage!" he said.

The toys hopped their pet carrier
onto the conveyor belt alongside Al's bag.
The belt carried them into a huge baggage area.
"Split up and start looking," cried Buzz.

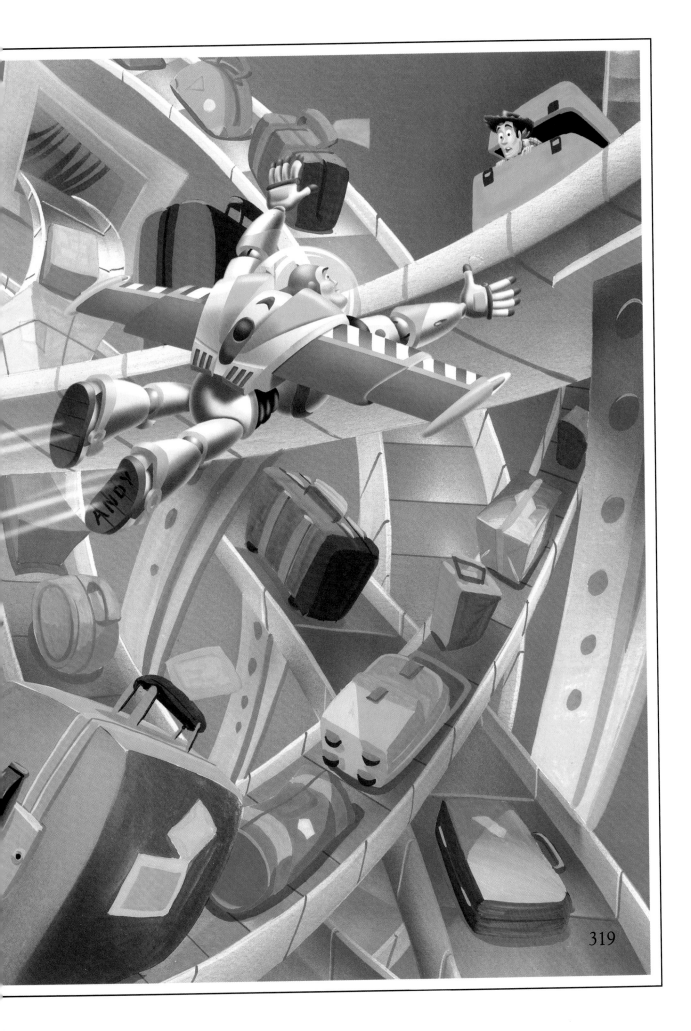

Opening one bag, Buzz found . . . an angry
Prospector! Woody escaped from his case and
helped Buzz stuff the Prospector into a passing
backpack.

Next, Bullseye struggled free from the case, but Jessie was still trapped inside. Woody and Buzz jumped onto Bullseye's back.

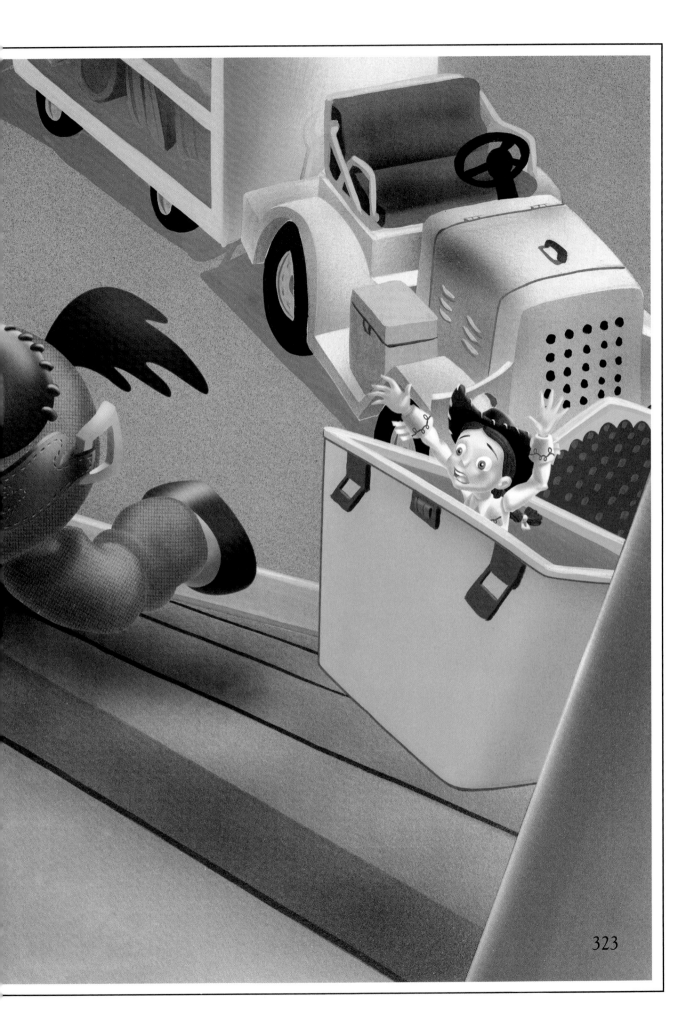

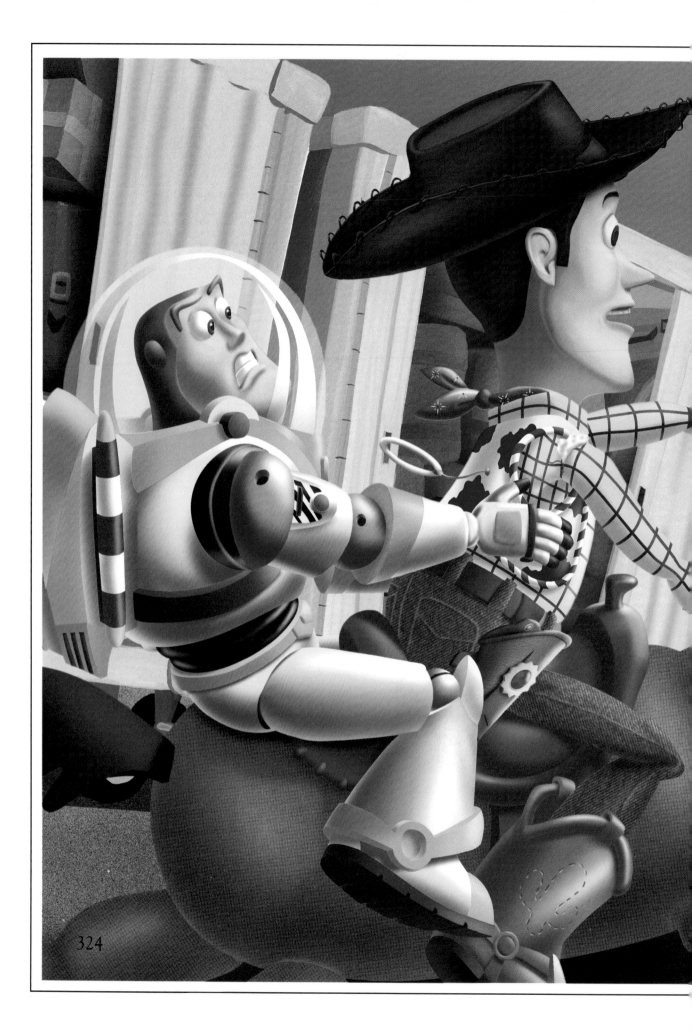

"Yee-hah! Giddy-up!" Woody shouted. Then he jumped from Bullseye's back to the baggage train that was carrying Jessie away.

But Woody wasn't able to rescue Jessie.
They were both loaded onto the plane—and
the plane was about to take off!

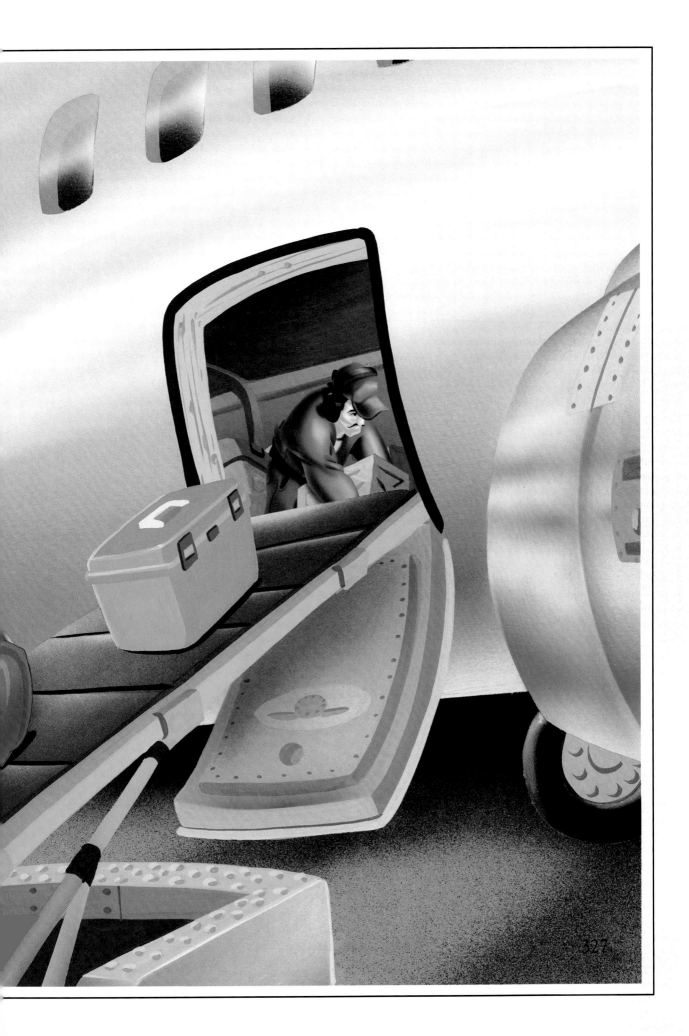

From inside the plane, Woody and Jessie tried to escape through the landing gear.

"You can't have a rescue without Buzz Lightyear," cried Buzz. He rode Bullseye under the plane—Woody and Jessie jumped to safety!

That evening, Andy returned. "What is that baggage carrier doing parked on the street?" wondered his mom.

332

Andy burst into his room. The first thing he did was look for Woody.

"Howdy, pardner!" he said. Then he spotted Bullseye and Jessie. "New toys! Thanks, Mom!" he cried.

And from that time on, Woody and his friends were happy not to be stuck on a museum shelf. They were real toys—played with and loved.

Disney's
The Fox and the Hound

❧ RETOLD BY MARCUS GAVE ❧

Tod and Copper

At the edge of a wood, Big Mama the owl found something small, red, and furry—a baby fox.

340

"I got an idea," said a sparrow named Dinky. Boomer the woodpecker pecked at the farmhouse door as Big Mama and Dinky flew off with Widow Tweed's laundry.

"Oh, you pesky birds!" the widow shouted, chasing them.

The birds led her to the kit. "You're such a little toddler," she said. "That's what I'm going to call you—Tod." She took her new friend home.

342

344

Next door, Amos Slade was just coming home. "I've got a surprise for you, Chief," he told his big old dog. Amos held up a hound puppy. "How's this for a hunting dog? He's for you to look after."

The puppy was called Copper.
One morning he found Tod playing
in the woods.

They began to play together. Before long, they decided they would be friends forever.

Then one day Copper did not show up to play. Tod went looking for him.

"Hey, Copper," Tod said. "What happened to you?" Then he saw Chief.

"Don't go in there," whispered Copper. But Tod was curious.

Chief was awake in no time. He chased Tod through the yard.

"Ruff, ruff!" he barked. Amos ran to the window just in time to see the fox and dog run by.

Racing toward home, Tod jumped up
alongside Widow Tweed, who was just
driving away.

Amos Slade was following in his car, shooting
at Tod.

Widow Tweed stood up to Amos. "That temper
of yours is going to get you into a lot of trouble
someday," she stormed.

Growing Up

Time has a way of changing things.

By the time winter had come and gone and spring had arrived, Tod was grown.

"Well, look who's here!" said Big Mama. "My goodness!"

Tod spied Amos Slade driving home. He and the dogs had been away hunting all winter.

"Copper's back!" Tod said to himself. "Boy, has he grown big. Copper's gonna be glad to see me."

Tod paid a call on his old friend.

"It's good to see you, Tod," said Copper, "but you shouldn't be over here."

"We're still friends, aren't we?" Tod asked.

"Those days are over," replied Copper sadly. "I'm a hunting dog now."

Tod didn't understand. Before he had a chance to say anything more, Chief awoke and lunged at Tod, barking loudly. Then, Slade appeared, shotgun in hand.

"There's that fox again!" he shouted.

Chief traced Tod's scent all the way to the railroad bridge. Amos followed as fast as he could, and now Copper came running up, too.

Tod could hear Chief behind him. Suddenly, a light pierced the darkness. A train was rumbling toward him!

Tod thought quickly. He flattened himself against the tracks and held his breath.

Chief, however, was too big for that. There was nothing he could do but jump.

Copper ran over to make sure his friend Chief was still alive. Looking up, Copper angrily said, "Tod, I'll . . . I'll get you for this!"

Back home, Chief rested his broken leg. Amos Slade and Copper saw Widow Tweed driving home.

"She dropped that fox off at the game preserve," Slade said. Tod was too big to live in the house anymore. "We'll get him!" The hunter showed Copper a scary trap.

Big Mama also knew that Tod had arrived at the game preserve. She thought she saw him, but it was Vixey, a female fox. Big Mama told Vixey all about Tod.

"I'll help you find him," said Vixey.

Big Mama and Vixey found Tod. He was all by himself, feeling sad.

"I just know you're going to love the forest," Vixey promised him. "I'll show you around."

Danger in the Woods

Amos Slade arrived at the game preserve, along with Copper and several traps.

Nearby, Vixey stopped, sensing danger.

"Tod, wait a minute," she said.

But Tod continued on. As traps snapped around him, Tod turned and ran. Slade and Copper were close on his trail.

Suddenly Copper was right in front of Tod.

"Grrr!" the hound growled.

The two fought until Tod got loose and ran away.
Copper and Slade were not far behind him.

Vixey was waiting for Tod.
They ran onto a fallen tree trunk
above a deep, deep gorge.
"We've trapped them now,
Copper," Slade said gleefully.

But before he could take one more step, a huge
bear appeared!

Stumbling backward, Amos felt his gun go
flying. Then, *snap!* One of his own traps locked
around his foot.

"Copper!" he shouted fearfully. The loyal
hound jumped at the bear, which swatted him
with a paw.

Tod and Vixey heard barking and snarling.
Tod headed back toward Copper.
"Tod!" shouted Vixey.

With little thought for his own safety, Tod jumped
onto the bear's back.

"Arrrgh!" growled the bear, flinging Tod through
the air and onto the rotting tree trunk over the
gorge.

The bear followed Tod onto the trunk. With a great swoop of its paw, it splintered the tree trunk.

Tod, the bear, and the tree toppled down, down, down into the gorge.

The bear landed with a thud and lay still. Tod could barely lift his head.

"Tod!" said Copper.

Suddenly Amos was there, gun in hand. Copper threw himself between the gun and his old friend.

"Well, c'mon, boy." Even Amos Slade could not be so heartless as to shoot the fox now.

"Let's go home," he said to his hound.

Before leaving, Copper turned to Tod. Neither of them had to say a word to know how the other felt.

397.

Back home, Widow Tweed bandaged the foot that Amos had caught in the trap.

"You'll soon be yourself," she said. "I don't know if I like that!"

399

From a nearby hill, Tod and Vixey looked down at the farmhouse. They knew they would be safe now.

Tod thought of the words he and Copper had spoken long ago: "We'll always be friends." He hoped Copper was thinking of them, too.